REUBEN AND THE QUILT
P. BUCKLEY MOSS, Artist
Story by MERLE GOOD

Intercourse, PA 17534 • 800/762-7171
www.goodbks.com

REUBEN AND THE QUILT
Text copyright © 1999 by Good Books, Intercoruse, PA 17534
Art copyright © 1999 by P. Buckley Moss
Design by Dawn J. Ranck
First published in 1999.
New Paperback edition published in 2002.
International Standard Book Number: 1-56148-354-0 (paperback)
International Standard Book Number: 1-56148-234-X (hardcover)
Library of Congress Catalog Card Number: 98-51953

Library of Congress Cataloging-in-Publication Data
Moss, P. Buckley (Pat Buckley)
    Reuben and the quilt / P. Buckley Moss, artist ; story by Merle
Good
    p. cm.
    Summary: Reuben and his Amish family make a beautiful Log
Cabin quilt to raise money for a sick neighbor, but then it is stolen
before they can take it to auction.
    ISBN: 1-56148-234-X (hc.). -- ISBN: 1-56148-354-0 (pbk.)
    [1. Quilts--Fiction. 2. Quilting--Fiction. 3. Amish--Fiction.]
I. Good, Merle. II. Title.
PZ7.M85355Rg 1998
[E]--dc21   98-51953
                                                                CIP
                                                                AC

One day, long before the quilt was ever stolen, Reuben was sweating in the strawberry patch, trying to fill his box with those yummy red things without eating them all.

To tell the truth, he was thinking about Splotch and Blotch, Sam and Ben's new puppies. Sam and Ben lived on the next farm. The twins were his best friends.

Suddenly a wet strawberry hit Reuben on the forehead.

He stood up fast and saw his sister Sadie trying to act normal, like she hadn't done anything. She was younger than Reuben, and could be quite a handful.

He couldn't decide whether to yell at her or to pitch a

strawberry fastball at her when Datt* stood up straight, right there in the middle of his row, and said, "A Log Cabin, maybe."

Reuben couldn't figure out what his father meant, but like usual, his mother seemed to.

"I know just the colors," Mamm* said.

*See final page for pronunciation.

It was all quilt talk, of course. So Reuben didn't pay any attention. He missed Sadie twice with a strawberry without his parents noticing, but then he landed a big, mushy one smack on her cheek.

"Quit it, Reuben!" she shouted.

But of course he had his face buried in the green leafy plants, looking for those ripe berries as though he had no idea what was happening around him. He knew Datt was watching him, so Reuben picked those strawberries as though it would break his heart to do anything else!

Later that night, over at the twins' hideaway behind the corn shed near the orchard, Reuben and Sam and Ben played with Splotch and Blotch.

Sam didn't seem very happy. "Our grandfather has to go back to the hospital again," he said to Reuben, rubbing the puppies' ears with the tall grass. "But we don't have the money. I'm worried."

Reuben figured out that's what gave Datt his idea about the Log Cabin quilt.

The twins' grandfather had been in a serious accident, when a car came around a corner, much too fast, and slammed into the back of his buggy.

Datt and some of the neighbors decided to have an auction to help pay for the expensive operation. And Datt was suggesting that he and Mamm and Reuben's five sisters—and maybe even Reuben himself—should make a quilt to sell at the auction. A Log Cabin quilt.

Reuben yawned. He was about as excited with the idea of a quilt as his pony Starshine was when he had to go out into the rain on a cold day. Not very, in other words.

Mamm came home from the store, delighted about the lively new quilt fabrics she had discovered. She pulled out her scrap bag and added some patches which looked like deep watercolors. Then she and Reuben's sisters, Annie, Mary, Barbie, Nancy, and Sadie, unwrapped the Log Cabin quilt pattern. They started cutting out pieces which looked like logs. Logs of many colors.

They marked the pattern on the fabric, log after log, cutting and sewing, log upon log, creating one beautiful quilt top. It seemed like so many log cabins when Reuben looked at the whole thing, each with a cozy fireplace in the center.

"The whole thing's boring," he said, even though he sort of liked to watch the pieces come together.

"A quilt is like an ice cream sandwich," Reuben's oldest sister Annie said. "The puffy batting in the middle is the ice cream, and the fabric is the top and bottom. The stitches hold it together."

"Where's the ice cream?" Reuben asked. "I'm hungry."

"Oh, go find something to do," Annie said. "Boys don't know anything about quilts and beauty." She was bossy that way.

But Mamm grabbed Reuben's arm as he went by. "Sit down here and put in a few stitches," she coaxed. "We are giving the quilt to your friends' grandfather. You should help a little."

Annie frowned, but Reuben sat.

It was the first time that Reuben quilted on a real quilt. He had made a few small, simple patches when he was younger, just for fun. But pushing a needle through such colorful fabric made him feel grown up. And a little nervous. He was scared he would prick himself.

"My stitches will probably be too big," he complained. He knew that good quilters made small, tight stitches.

"You're doing fine," Mamm said.

His sisters laughed. "We can always pull out his stitches and do them right," Sadie giggled.

"No, you won't," Dawdi* warned from the corner. "If Reuben's careful and does his best, no one should take out his stitches," his grandfather said.

*See final page for pronunciation.

The morning after they finished the quilt, it disappeared. None of Reuben's family understood how the quilt was stolen. Reuben had never heard of such a thing. Annie said it was Nancy's fault, but Nancy was sure she had brought the quilt back into the house.

"I just wanted to see it while I mowed the lawn," she said. "I hung it on the porch. It's such a lovely quilt, and we only had a few days to enjoy it before it would be sold at the auction. Now we'll probably never see it again."

"We'll never see it again, that's for sure," Mamm sighed. "What kind of world do we live in where people steal quilts off other people's porches?"

But Datt was a forgiving man. "Maybe the thief is really poor and needed it," he said after breakfast.

The whole thing made Annie very grouchy. "We even sewed pillow cases to match," she muttered. "A bunch of stolen time, that's what!"

It was a less than happy day. Reuben hoped Sam and Ben wouldn't come over to see him, because he didn't want to tell them the bad news.

"All my careful stitching was a waste," he said to Mamm as they shelled peas on the porch.

"Maybe whoever took it will return it," his mother said. But he knew she was upset from the way she tossed the pods into the basket.

Then Datt got another of his crazy ideas. Even Dawdi was surprised.

"Let's put the two pillow cases in a bag and set them out on the picnic table by the road," Datt said.

"Whatever for?" Annie asked.

"If the thief is really needy, he'll have to have something to lay his head on when he's sleeping under our quilt," Datt said.

"Yeah, what if he's just greedy instead of needy?" Reuben asked.

"Then we'll forgive him. We can always make another quilt."

"Not before the auction," Annie groaned.

"Sometimes if you turn the other cheek, it brings out the best in others," Datt said.

Reuben couldn't go to sleep that night. He kept crawling out of bed, very quietly, so his parents wouldn't hear him walking across the floor. He went to the window and watched the road. The moon was almost full, and he could faintly see the bag on the picnic table.

They had put a sign on the bag, "To the Quilt-Taker," it read. "Here are two pillow cases which match."

Reuben wasn't sure he believed in this "other cheek" stuff. "It feels like we're rewarding someone who robbed us," he complained to Dawdi before he went to bed.

"It's wrong to steal," Dawdi said. "But how we respond can also be wrong."

Reuben watched the road as long as he could. Finally he crawled into bed and fell asleep.

The next morning, the bag with the two pillow cases was back on the porch, along with another large sack.

Reuben opened the big sack carefully. He couldn't believe what he saw. "They brought the quilt back!" he yelled to his father. He pulled the beautiful Log Cabin out of the bag as his

sisters came running out of the house. Everyone was amazed. Even Annie didn't know what to say.

But Datt just stroked his beard and smiled that half grin of his at Mamm.

The next week, dozens of neighbors came for the auction. It was a splendid June day, bright sunshine, breeze in the trees, and the smell of freshly cut hay.

Reuben helped Sam and Ben carry things for the auctioneer. They got so busy they hardly had time to eat, but Mamm brought them each a piece of the cherry pie when she saw how hard they were working.

Several quilts had been donated to the auction. Reuben liked watching them sell, trying to guess which person would offer the most money for each quilt. But it was the Log Cabin made by his family which brought the highest price.

Mr. Ober, who owned the grocery store, gave the top bid. "That's a good price," Dawdi smiled. "That will help with the hospital costs."

Mr. Ober seldom smiled. Reuben knew that's why people called him "Sober Ober."

But today he almost beamed as he walked toward Sam and Ben, carrying the Log Cabin quilt. "I bought this for your grandfather," he told the twins. "The money will help with the operation. But the quilt is so beautiful, I think he should have it, too, to keep him warm and to cheer him up."

Reuben heard Mamm sigh that deep sound she made when she was very happy. "Sometimes when we decide to help others, there's no telling how much good will come of it," she smiled.

And Reuben smiled, too. It was the first quilt he had helped to make.

Those logs had never looked more colorful and grand than they did as Sam and Ben took the quilt from Sober Ober. Every color in the rainbow sparkled from the fabrics as the twins headed up the porch steps to give the quilt to their grandfather.

Everyone was satisfied. Even Reuben's sister Annie smiled. "Now you can see the Log Cabin whenever you visit your friends," she said.

Note

There are approximately 150,000 Old Order Amish persons, including children, living in 22 states and one province in North America. Reuben's family in this story is typical of the Amish in Lancaster County, Pennsylvania.

The religious beliefs of the Amish teach them to be cautious about many modern innovations, such as automobiles, electricity, telephones, television, and higher education. They observe that these modern things often fragment people's lives and relationships more than they fulfill them. For 300 years, Amish communities have sought a "separate way," emphasizing family, honesty, basic values, and faith.

For more information about the Amish, write to or visit The People's Place, P.O. Box 419, Intercourse, PA 17534 (along Route 340), an Amish and Mennonite heritage center (of which Merle Good and his wife Phyllis are Executive Directors). Or request a free list of books about the Amish.

About the Artist

P. Buckley Moss (Pat) first met the Amish in 1965 when she and her family moved to Waynesboro in the Shenandoah Valley of Virginia. Admiring the family values and work ethic of her new neighbors, Pat began to include the Amish in her paintings.

Many of her paintings and etchings of both the Amish and the Old Order Mennonites are displayed at the P. Buckley Moss Museum in Waynesboro, which is open to the public throughout the year. For more information, write to: The Director, P. Buckley Moss Museum, 2150 Rosser Avenue, Waynesboro, VA 22980.

Moss and Good collaborated on the earlier classic children's books, *Reuben and the Fire* and *Reuben and the Blizzard.*

About the Author

Merle Good has written numerous books and articles about the Amish, including Op-Ed essays for the *New York Times* and the beautiful book *Who Are the Amish?* In addition to The People's Place, he and his wife Phyllis oversee a series of projects in publishing and the arts. Merle and Phyllis Good have also co-authored several books, including *20 Most Asked Questions About the Amish and Mennonites* and *Christmas Ideas for Families.* They live in Lancaster, Pennsylvania, and are the parents of two daughters.